SING A SONG OF SIXPENCE

SING A SONG OF SIXPENCE

BARRON'S

First edition for the United States
published 1988 by Barron's
Educational Series, Inc.

Copyright © in this edition
Century Hutchinson Ltd 1987

First published 1987 by
Hutchinson Children's Books
An imprint of Century Hutchinson Ltd
London, England

All inquiries should be addressed to:
Barron's Educational Series, Inc.
250 Wireless Boulevard
Hauppauge, New York 11788

Library of Congress Catalog Card No. 87–18829
International Standard Book No. 0–8120–5900–X

Printed in Italy

789 9680 987654321

SING A SONG OF SIXPENCE

ILLUSTRATED BY
RANDOLPH CALDECOTT

SERIES EDITOR · ELIZABETH RUDD

BARRON'S

NEW YORK

Sing a song of sixpence,
A pocket full of rye;

F our-and-twenty blackbirds,
Baked in a pie.

W hen the pie was opened,
The birds began to sing.

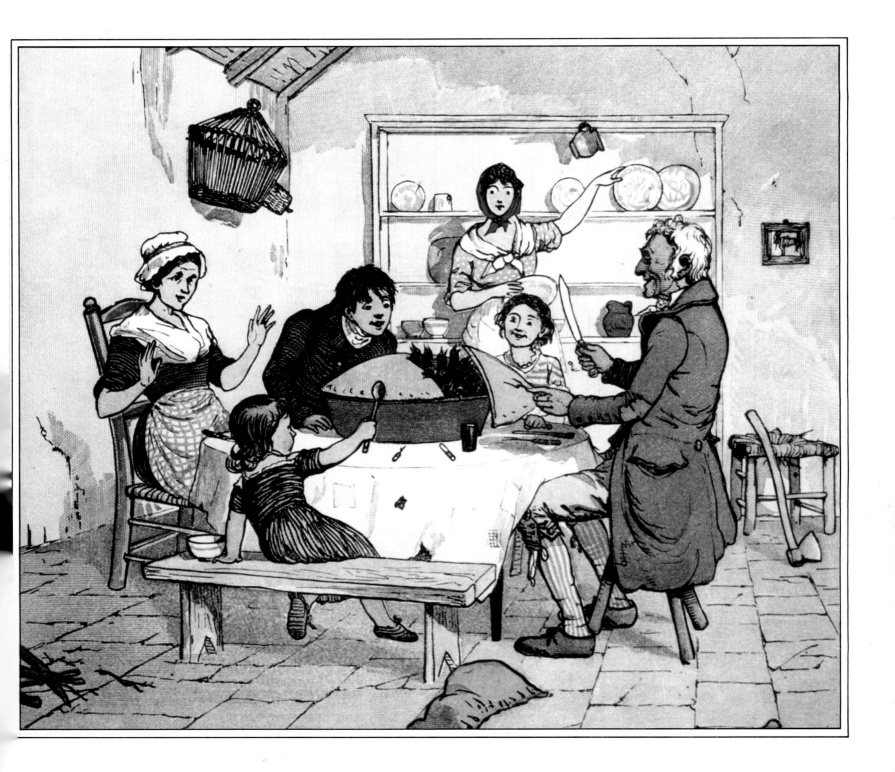

W asn't that a dainty dish,
To set before the king?

The king was in his counting house,
Counting out his money;

The queen was in the parlor,
Eating bread and honey;

T he maid was in the garden
Hanging out the clothes,

W hen down came a blackbird
And snipped off her nose.

$$B$$ut then there came a little wren
And popped it on again.